Molly *and the* Sword

Written by Robert Shlasko
Illustrated by Donna Diamond

Jane & Street Publishers Ltd.
New York

Jane & Street Publishers Ltd.
New York, N.Y.

www.janeandstreet.com

The illustrations for this book were done on paper.
They were painted with a brush and colored inks over
sepia line drawings made with an antique crow quill pen.

Designed by Sharon Murray Jacobs.
Text set in fourteen-point Weiss Regular and Italic.
Printed on acid-free paper by Berryville Graphics, Inc. in the United States of America.
Library of Congress Control Number: 2003112249

ISBN 0-9745077-4-1

First Printing

1   3   5   7   9   10   8   6   4   2

To Gabrielle
(who shares a birthday with her great grandmother Molly),
Sara and Leora

. . . and to brave girls
everywhere!

For as long as she could remember, life in her village seemed so wonderful to Molly. There was no hint of what was to come.

Day after day, Molly listened with joy as her mother sang, filling the air with beautiful music. With her mother, she kept busy working in their vegetable garden. All the while, she kept an eye on her younger brother and sister to see that they stayed out of trouble.

Whenever she could, Molly also helped her father in his shop. It was there that he made marvelous clocks.

How Molly loved her happy family.

Alas, one day there was a great change in the village — for a war had begun. A war with the country to the north. (This was long ago, a time when countries were quick to argue — and, foolishly, quick to fight.)

Within a few weeks, enemy soldiers were in the nearby countryside. Soon, the sound of musket fire filled the air.

As the fighting continued, Molly's family faced a serious problem: Their well had run dry.

Molly knew her mother was expecting a new baby. She was certain life would become difficult if they went without water much longer.

Molly's father looked so worried. How she wished she could help!

Her mother tried to comfort him. "The well in the village square is much deeper," she said. "As soon as the fighting stops, we can go there and get all the water we need."

Her father made a decision. Standing up, he declared, "I must go to the square."

Alarmed, Molly's mother protested, "You can't. It's too dangerous."

Molly watched wide-eyed. She thought very hard. Then she
stepped forward.

"Father," she said firmly, "Mother and the children need you.
What if something were to happen on the way to the well?
No, I will go!"

Her father looked at her with tears in his eyes. "My brave little
Molly," he said. He shook his head: "I could never let you do that."

Molly's father paced up and down as he and his wife
discussed what to do. Suddenly, they stopped in alarm. The side
door had just clicked shut. Then they heard footsteps rushing
away from the house.

Looking around, they realized the water pail was gone and
with it — Molly.

She was going to the well. And it was too late to stop her!

utside, Molly hurried along seeking shelter behind houses and trees. From time to time, she heard the sound of musket shots in the distance.

Soon, she reached the village square. She took a deep breath, moved into the open and slowly made her way to the well.

Just as she prepared to lower her pail into the water, two enemy soldiers, one tall, one short, entered the square and ran toward her.

"Stop!" they shouted.

When they reached her, the tall one demanded, "What are you doing here?"

Nervous as she was, Molly noticed that the soldiers were nervous too. They were young and their uniforms were dirty from long days of fighting.

"I've come to get water from the well," Molly explained.

The soldiers glanced around uneasily. Then the short soldier said accusingly, "I think you're a spy."

Molly started to protest. But he pointed his musket at her and said, "Put down that pail and come with us."

Before she could respond, they heard hoofbeats approaching. An officer in the enemy army rode up on a beautiful white horse and quickly dismounted.

Like the soldiers, he was young. And his splendid uniform had rows of medals pinned to it. Molly looked at his handsome face and wondered: Did she see kindness there?

The two soldiers saluted as the officer asked, "What's going on here?"

"We've caught a spy, sir," the tall soldier replied.

The officer turned to Molly: "Is that true? Is that what you are?"

She straightened her back, lifted her chin high, and said, "I most certainly am *not* a spy."

The officer looked at her carefully before asking, "Then why are you here?"

"I've come for water."

"In the middle of a battle?"

Molly explained how much her family needed the water — and why she decided to come on her own.

The officer listened and nodded.

When she finished, he asked gently, "What is your name?"

Molly told him her full name, which he seemed to note carefully.

The officer was thoughtful. He looked into the eyes of the courageous girl standing in front of him.

Then he turned to the two soldiers and said, "I'm sure this girl is no spy." Reaching to his side, he pulled out a gleaming sword. Its beautiful handle was made of jewels, gold and ivory.

The officer went on, "Whoever harms her shall answer to me! Help her with the water. And see that she gets home safely."

Leaping back onto his horse, he rode away.

The two soldiers quickly obeyed his command.

How relieved Molly's family was when she came home unharmed! Her mother and father marveled at the courage of their daughter.

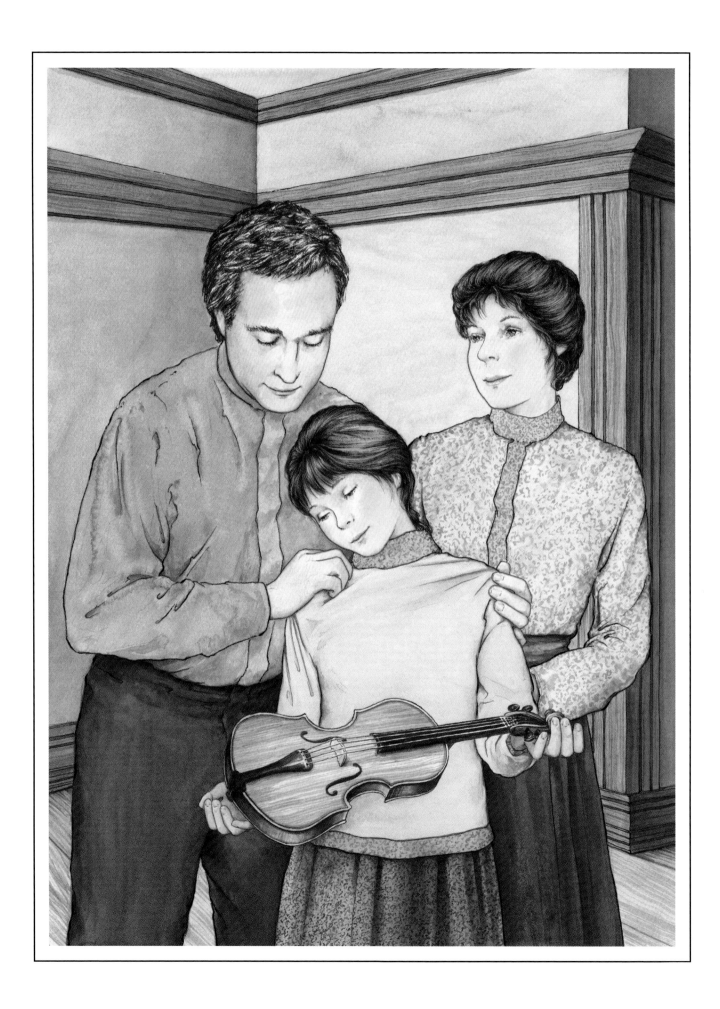

ime went by and the war ended. One sign of peace was the arrival in the village of a traveling circus. Molly sat in the audience with her family, enjoying every moment.

Most of all, she was enchanted by a clown who danced around the circus ring playing a violin. The more he played, the more Molly loved the music.

On the way home, she talked endlessly about the sound of the wonderful violin.

Soon it was Molly's birthday. Her parents wanted to do something special for her. They remembered how the clown's music had thrilled her.

Her father took his most beautiful clock, went to a neighboring town and came back with a gift — a violin.

Molly was so excited. She could hardly wait to start playing.

There was a musician in the village and he began giving her lessons. Molly worked so hard and learned so fast that soon the musician said, "It's time to find someone who can help you further."

He sent her to a famous teacher in the city. This teacher had students from far and wide. He took one look at her and said scornfully, "I don't have time to waste on girls. I only teach serious violinists." (This teacher loved music . . . but in those days many people felt as he did about girls.)

Someone else might have fled at his fierce words. Not Molly! She was angry and she said, "That's not fair. I've come a long way. You should at least listen."

The teacher looked up, surprised by her spirit. He said with a sigh, "Very well, let me hear you play — then go home."

As Molly raised the violin to her chin, the teacher started to read his newspaper. Molly began to play. Soon, the teacher put down his paper and listened more carefully.

When Molly finished, he stood — silent. Finally, he said, "Well, I'm still not sure I like the idea, but perhaps a few lessons wouldn't hurt. Mind you, just a few!"

Those few lessons stretched into years of study.

Then, with the help of her teacher, Molly was invited to play her violin in a small music hall.

She was such a success that soon halls in other cities asked her to play. Her sister Clara, who had learned the piano, came to join her. The two girls even traveled to small music halls in other lands.

Molly was happy because she was playing her beloved violin. But Clara wondered why the big music halls would still not accept Molly. Was it because she was a girl?

"When," asked Clara, "will you get the chance you deserve?" She added, "Your teacher is annoyed too. He wants to see that you are treated fairly."

ne day, unexpectedly, a letter arrived.

It was from the country to the north.

That country had the most famous music hall in all the world. The letter invited Molly to play in the hall.

Overjoyed, she practiced and practiced. Finally, the big night arrived. In a room backstage, her sister watched as Molly paced nervously back and forth.

"Oh, Clara," said Molly, "why did I agree to come? There are so many people out there. Perhaps, I'm not good enough."

"Nonsense, Molly. You play wonderfully. The audience will love you."

"But what if they don't? I've never been this worried. How can I go on? The way I feel, I can't play well."

Just then there was a knock on the door. Clara opened it and in walked a man in a handsome uniform. He was a Royal Messenger, and he was carrying a large package. Standing erect, he announced to Molly: "My orders are to see that you receive this personally."

All eyes were on her as she unwrapped the package. Molly gasped when she saw what was in it. Although many years had passed, she immediately recognized the glittering sword. It was the one carried by the officer on the white horse — the officer who had saved her at the village well.

Then the Royal Messenger removed a note from his pocket and said, "I was told to give you this too."

Clara took the note from Molly's shaking hand and read it aloud: "To the bravest person I have ever met."

Molly felt her face redden with embarrassment. Then she took a deep breath and threw back her head. Smiling, she said calmly to Clara, "It's time for the concert to begin."

She walked on stage. The audience stirred as up in the royal box, the Prince of the kingdom rose to his feet and bowed to Molly.

She knew him at once. He was the officer at the well. Molly bowed to him, and lifting her violin to her chin began to play as she had never played before.

A golden sound, pure and sweet, filled the hall. The music was so beautiful! Molly played on. As they listened, the people in the audience knew that in years to come, they would tell their children and their grandchildren about this magical day.

Molly finished playing and the people cheered wildly. She raised her eyes to the royal box.

Like the rest of the audience, the Prince rose to his feet. He looked at the girl who, in a village square, had taught him a valuable lesson: Courage shows itself in many ways — not just in fighting. The Prince smiled and bowed to her again.

Molly looked at the man who had taught her that an enemy could become a friend. She smiled and bowed to him.

And the audience continued to applaud and cheer.

The End